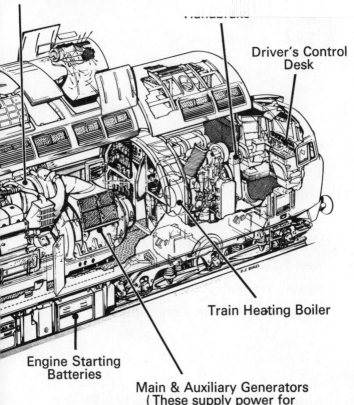

Turbo Charger
(boosts air supply to engine)

Handbrake

Driver's Control
Desk

Train Heating Boiler

Engine Starting
Batteries

Main & Auxiliary Generators
(These supply power for
driving motors, etc.)

MAIN LINE 2,750 H.P.
DIESEL-ELECTRIC LOCOMOTIVE
Designed and built by
The Brush Electrical Engineering Co. Ltd.

Series 654
A Ladybird Book

Steam locomotives have virtually left the railway scene: modern diesel and electric locomotives have taken their place. How do these latest monarchs of the railways work? How do the men in the driving cabs control them? This book will give you many of the answers and make your future train spotting or travelling all the more interesting.

We wish to acknowledge the assistance of British Railways and Mr. K. E. LIMBERT, C.ENG., M.I.D.E., A.M.I.LOCO.E. when preparing this book.

'How it works'
THE LOCOMOTIVE
Diesel and Electric

by DAVID CAREY

with illustrations by B. H. ROBINSON

Publishers Wills & Hepworth Ltd., Loughborough
First published 1968   ©   *Printed in England*

The Great Change

The big steam locomotives which have drawn our famous trains for about one hundred and fifty years, have now given way to locomotives propelled by diesel and electric power. Many railway enthusiasts will regret the passing of the steam engine with its very individual character, its impressive appearance, its powerful beat and its distinctive whistle.

Modern diesel or electric locomotives do not seem to have the same special attraction, yet they are more efficient in operation, quieter, cleaner, more economical to run and faster between stations than their more glamorous predecessors. And, of course, it is for the travellers rather than the enthusiasts that the railways must be run. Train spotters of the future will know nothing of the steam age which is rapidly receding into history.

How do these latest monarchs of the railways pull their heavy loads of carriages, passengers and goods along the iron highways of the world? How do the men in the driving cabs control them? This book will give you many of the answers and make your future spotting or travelling all the more interesting.

The diesel locomotive is dealt with in the first part of the book, followed by the electric locomotive toward the end. They have features of great difference as well as certain similarities.

4

7214 0225 9

The Diesel Locomotive Power Plant

All diesel locomotives have a diesel engine which provides the power to drive the locomotive which pulls the train.

Every diesel engine has *cylinders*, which are really tubes bored out of a cylinder block and closed off at the top by the cylinder head. In each cylinder a *piston* slides up and down. Instead of the piston working directly against the metal of the cylinder block, liners are fitted, made of special material better able to withstand wear and tear and corrosion. These can be more easily and cheaply replaced than the whole cylinder block.

The movement of a piston up and down a cylinder is called a *stroke*. Pistons are joined to a *connecting rod*, the lower end of which is connected to a *crankshaft*. The crankshaft is shaped so that as the pistons move up and down they cause it to revolve. The action is the same as someone riding a bicycle: his knees are the pistons, his legs the connecting rods and his feet on the pedals, the crankshaft. The turning movement of the crankshaft provides the power to drive the locomotive along.

Around each piston there are a number of cast iron *piston rings*. All the piston rings are split and act as springs, pushing against the walls of the cylinder liner, sealing the space in the cylinder above the piston from the area below.

Some diesel engines are fitted with valves, two or more for each cylinder, inlet valves and outlet valves in equal numbers. These are opened and closed by *push rods* and the action of *cams*, or projections, on the camshaft.

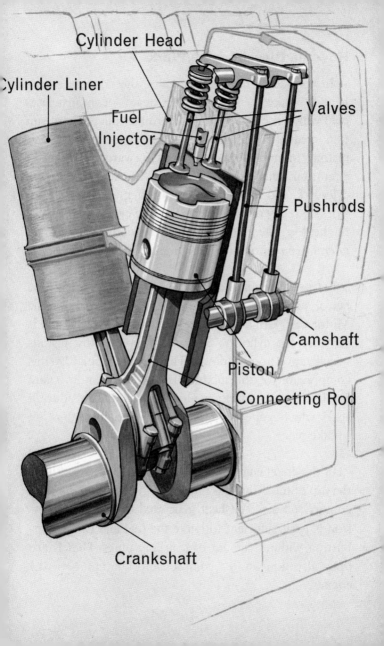

Cylinder Head

Cylinder Liner

Fuel Injector

Valves

Pushrods

Camshaft

Piston

Connecting Rod

Crankshaft

How the Diesel Engine Works

In common with steam engines, diesel engines need heat to make them work. The steam locomotive uses coal which is burnt to heat water in a boiler. The steam thus created is then fed into the cylinders and causes pistons to move backward and forward. With diesel operation, the necessary heat is created *within* the cylinders and the resulting burning, or *combustion*, works directly on the pistons in these cylinders. Because the heat is generated internally the diesel is known as an *internal combustion* (or i.c.) engine.

Let us make another comparison, this time with the petrol engine of a car, (see, "How it Works—The Motor Car"). In a car engine, a petrol and air mixture is fed into the cylinders and is compressed by pistons which move up and down. The heat generated by this compression of the mixture is not sufficient to cause combustion, so sparking plugs are used to produce a spark which ignites the mixture and enables combustion to take place.

In the diesel engine, air is compressed by pistons into the top of the cylinders. Fuel oil is then sprayed into the compressed air. The heat generated through compression is itself sufficient to ignite the fuel and cause combustion without the aid of sparking plugs. Diesels are thus also known as compression ignition (or c.i.) engines.

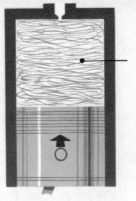

Cold air being compressed

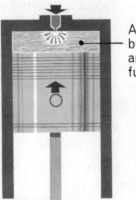

Air heated by compression and fuel sprayed in

Combustion drives piston down

The Miracle of Combustion

We have seen how fuel is sprayed into the compressed air at the top of the cylinder to enable combustion to take place. The space in which this occurs is known as the combustion chamber, and, in a diesel engine, its design is very important. The power that is developed by the engine depends on efficient combustion occurring to drive the piston forcibly down the cylinder and give the crankshaft a powerful turning movement, or *torque*. Efficient combustion depends to a great extent on the complete inter-mixing of the fuel spray with the air under compression in the cylinder. It is therefore necessary to design the combustion chamber and the top of the piston (the piston crown) in such a way that the air is given a strong swirling motion as it is being compressed. This swirling motion helps the mixing process, which, of course, must take place in a tiny fraction of a second.

The type of diesel engine we have described is known as a *direct injection* engine because the fuel is sprayed directly into the top of the cylinder where combustion takes place. In another type of engine, a separate swirl chamber is used to mix the fuel with the air. Combustion takes place in this chamber and the expanding gases then force themselves into the cylinder to drive the piston down. This system is called *indirect injection*.

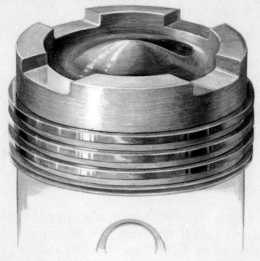

Piston Crown

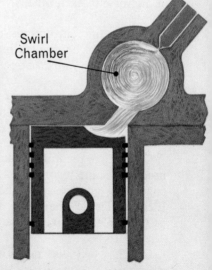

Swirl
Chamber

Direct Injection
Air given swirling motion
before fuel injection

Indirect Injection
Air and fuel, mixed in
separate swirl chamber

The Ways in which Diesel Engines vary

Locomotive diesel engines vary in shape, size and power. The number and the arrangement of the cylinders also varies. Thus there are many different designs of diesel engines.

One rather special design is the '*deltic*' engine. In this engine the cylinders are placed in triangular formation, each cylinder having two pistons working in opposite directions.

Then there are *in-line* engines of six or eight cylinders, placed one behind the other. For more power twelve cylinders can be used. These are often arranged in two rows of six cylinders placed side by side. V engines are also employed, in which the cylinders are set in two rows at an angle to each other in 'V' formation.

All the different designs and shapes of diesel engine can, however, be divided into one of two basic types: *Four-stroke* or *Two-stroke*.

Four-stroke engines work on what is called the four-stroke cycle of operation, and two-stroke engines work on the two-stroke cycle of operation.

Of the two, the four-stroke cycle is the more generally used, but some locomotives are powered by two-stroke engines, a good example being the 3,300 h.p. English Electric 'Deltic' main-line diesel locomotive, powered by two 1,650 h.p. two-stroke engines of the deltic design.

On the next two pages we shall explain the four-stroke and two-stroke cycles of operation.

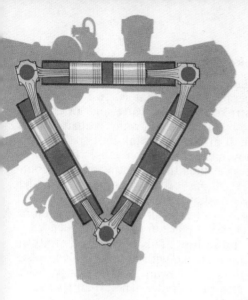

Deltic

Single-Bank
In-Line

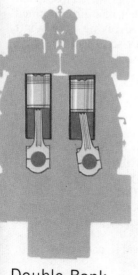

Double-Bank
In-Line

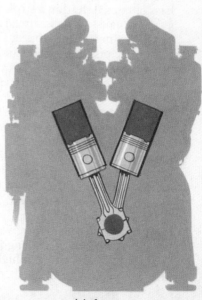

V-form

The Four-Stroke Cycle of Operation

In a four-stroke engine, four strokes of each piston complete the operating cycle: that is, two up strokes and two down strokes. An inlet valve and an exhaust valve are actuated by the camshaft, which is chain-driven from the crankshaft at half the crankshaft speed. Each up and down movement of a piston causes the crankshaft to revolve once, thus the operating cycle is completed in two revolutions of the crankshaft and one revolution of the camshaft.

Each of the four strokes, which are described more fully below, always takes place in the same sequence.

First stroke—Induction. This begins as the piston commences the down stroke with the inlet valve open. As the piston continues downward, it draws air past the open inlet valve into the cylinder. The exhaust valve is closed at this stage.

Second stroke—Compression. When the piston has completed the down stroke, the inlet valve closes, and as the exhaust valve is already closed, the air contained in the cylinder is trapped. The revolving crankshaft pushes the piston up again and as it rises, the air trapped in the cylinder is compressed up into the *combustion chamber*. As the air is compressed, it becomes extremely hot.

Third stroke—Power. With the valves still closed, fuel oil is sprayed through an *injector* into the top of the cylinder at the point of greatest compression and greatest heat. The heat of the air causes the fine oil spray to ignite and the resulting terrific expansion of the gases drives the piston down the cylinder.

Fourth stroke—Exhaust. At the end of the power stroke, the exhaust valve opens and, during the following up-stroke of the piston the waste gases are pushed past the valve and out of the engine.

This cycle is repeated at high speed in each cylinder in turn as long as the engine is running.

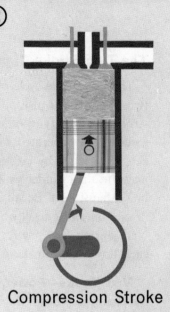

Induction Stroke

Compression Stroke

Fuel Injection ②

Waste Gases

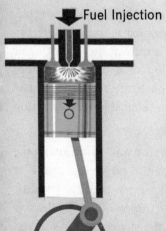

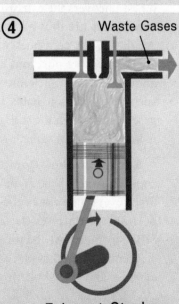

Power Stroke

Exhaust Stroke

The Two-Stroke Cycle of Operation

The two-stroke cycle of operation takes place during two strokes of a piston, one up stroke and one down stroke. In this type of engine there are normally no mechanically operated valves. Instead, the piston itself acts as a valve by covering and uncovering holes, or *ports*, in the cylinder walls. There is one inlet port and one exhaust port. Because the whole cycle is completed in one up and one down stroke of the piston, it takes place during only one revolution of the crankshaft, and each downward stroke is a power stroke.

First Stroke—Power, Exhaust and Induction. As the piston goes down the cylinder following combustion, it first uncovers the exhaust port. Some of the expanding waste gases are thus allowed to escape from the engine. As the piston continues downward it immediately uncovers the inlet port and air is drawn into the cylinder above the piston. The incoming air is made to swirl in such a way that it helps to push the remaining waste gases out through the still open exhaust port. This action is known as *scavenging*.

Second stroke—Compression and Ignition. As the crankshaft revolves, it pushes the piston up again. It first covers and closes the inlet port, then the exhaust port and compresses the now trapped air into the top of the cylinder. At the top of the stroke, fuel is sprayed in, combustion takes place, the piston is driven down the cylinder and the whole process is repeated.

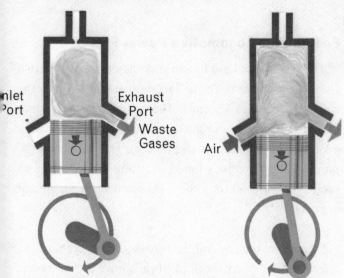

First Stroke – Power, Exhaust and Induction

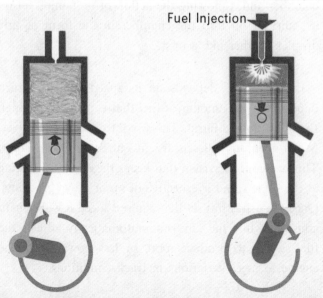

Second Stroke – Compression and Ignition

Fuelling the Locomotive Power Plant

The fuel oil used in a locomotive diesel engine is drawn from a storage tank in the locomotive and fed into the engine by means of pumps. There is usually one pump for each cylinder, mounted either separately or in a group at one point on the engine. The action of the pumps is very precisely timed to ensure that oil is fed to each cylinder at exactly the right moment in the operating cycle.

From the pumps, oil is forced under pressure to *injectors* fitted into the cylinder head above each cylinder. The injector nozzle protrudes into the combustion chamber and, following the action of its pump, sprays a squirt of oil into the chamber in the form of tiny droplets, rather like a mist.

Engine power depends on its speed, which in turn depends on the amount of fuel that is pumped through the injectors and burnt. This is controlled by the driver. Most locomotive diesels are also fitted with a *governor*. This is a control system that keeps the engine operating at the same speed irrespective of up or down gradients. Once the driver has set the required speed it will remain constant while the governor automatically adjusts the fuel supply to produce more or less power from the engine to meet variations in track conditions.

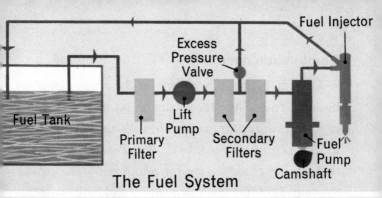

The Fuel System

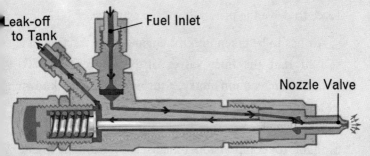

Fuel Injector

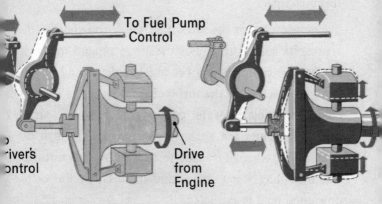

Speed setting by driver — maintained by governor

Speed Governor

Combustion needs Air—how it is supplied

Air is an essential ingredient for the process of combustion. To produce the maximum power from a given engine, it is necessary to get as much air as possible as quickly as possible into the cylinders, because the greater the quantity of air there is for compression, the greater the amount of fuel that can be burnt and the greater the force to drive the piston down the cylinder.

Air has to be taken into the engine in the fraction of a second that the inlet valves or ports are open. To obtain the maximum intake, a turbine-driven fan known as a *turbo-charger* is fitted. This blows the air into the cylinders under pressure, and so increases the quantity available for compression. Exhaust gases from the engine usually provide the means to drive the turbine of the turbo-charger.

Compression of the air within the turbo-charger increases its heat. This causes the air to expand before it reaches the cylinders and become less dense and, therefore, less useful. So the turbo-charger casing is kept as cold as possible by water cooling, or before the air is allowed to enter the engine it is first sent through an *inter-cooler*, where it is made to pass over pipes through which cooling water flows, and in this way the extra unwanted heat is extracted.

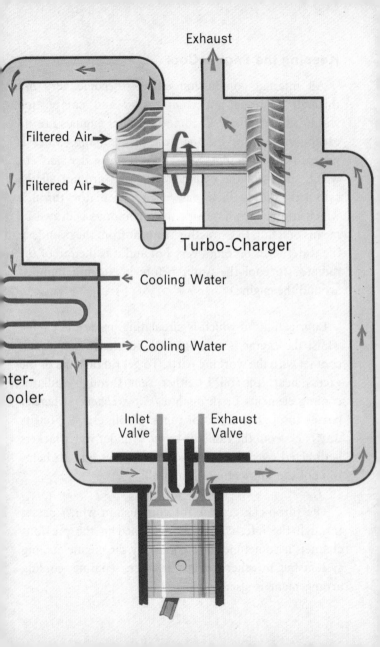

Exhaust

Filtered Air →

Filtered Air →

Turbo-Charger

← Cooling Water

→ Cooling Water

nter-
ooler

Inlet
Valve

Exhaust
Valve

Keeping the Engine Cool

All internal combustion engines become very hot through continual air compression and combustion within the cylinders. Locomotive diesel engines are no exception. To provide the necessary cooling, water is pumped through passages, known as *water jackets*, which surround the cylinders. It flows around all the cylinders and is then passed to a radiator through which cool air from outside the locomotive is drawn by means of a fan. In extracting the heat from the cylinders, the water itself becomes very hot and it is the job of the radiator to cool the water before it is again pumped around the engine.

Lubricating oil which is circulating inside the engine whilst the engine is running, also becomes hot through contact with the working parts. To get rid of some of the excess heat, the oil is either sent through radiator cooling elements or through a *heat-exchanger* where it passes through a series of pipes. Cooling water on its way back from the radiator to the cylinder water jackets is directed over the heat-exchanger pipes and so helps to cool the lubricating oil as well.

The turbo-charged air for combustion which passes through the inter-cooler, as described in the previous chapter, is sometimes also cooled by the engine cooling system but in other designs another, separate, cooling arrangement is used.

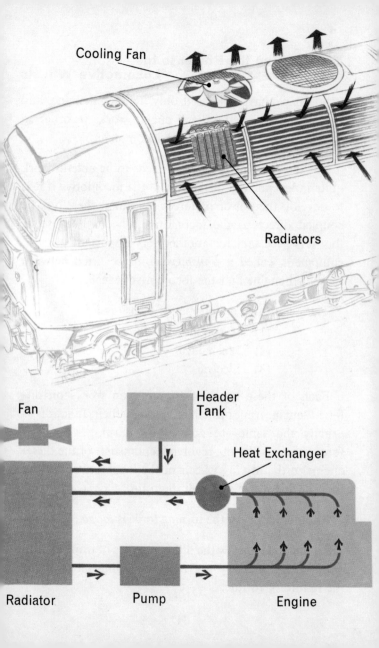

Cooling Fan

Radiators

Fan

Header Tank

Heat Exchanger

Radiator

Pump

Engine

Transmitting the Power to the Locomotive Wheels

So far we have discussed only the diesel engine, and the way in which the diesel engine works in order to provide the power to drive the locomotive.

The diesel engine, however, needs to be able to work quite independently of the rest of the locomotive if it is to develop the power required. It cannot, therefore, be coupled direct to the locomotive wheels. Because of this, it is necessary for another very important piece of equipment, called a *transmission*, to be fitted between the diesel engine and the locomotive wheels.

There are three main types of transmission:

    (1)   Hydraulic
    (2)   Mechanical
    (3)   Electric.

Each of these types of transmission works on different engineering principles, though their function is exactly the same—to convey the turning power or force produced by the revolving crankshaft of the diesel engine to the driving wheels of the locomotive, causing the wheels to turn and pull the train.

Another name for the turning force is *torque*.

To understand how the different types of transmission work, it is necessary to know something more about the nature of torque.

2,700 h.p.
Western Class
Diesel Locomotive
with hydraulic
transmission

A 3,300 h.p. Deltic
Diesel Locomotive
with electric
transmission

The Mystery of Torque

When you press down on the pedals of a bicycle, you are producing a turning force, or torque. It is a useful force which is transmitted to the rear wheel by means of a chain and enables you to propel the machine along. You will need a greater, or higher torque to start with in order to overcome the weight of yourself on the bicycle and the resistance of the tyres against the road. Once you get going, less force (torque) is required at the pedals, but you can now go faster. When you come to a hill or gradient, more torque is again required to cycle up it. At the top you can ease off once more.

In the same way, because of its weight, a train needs a high torque to start it off. As the speed increases less torque is required. When the train meets an up-gradient along the journey, more torque is needed again.

The driver of the locomotive, unlike the bicycle rider, cannot make the adjustments required in the torque to meet the varying road conditions, but luckily the transmission does this for him, usually without him being aware of it.

Now let us take a closer look at the three different types of transmission.

Hydraulic Transmission

The essential features of a hydraulic transmission is the *torque converter*.

The torque converter is rather like a hydraulic pump revolving inside a housing filled with oil. It has three main parts, of which two rotate and one is fixed. Each part consists of a ring with specially-shaped blades. The blades are curved to control the direction of the flow of oil.

The three main parts of a torque converter are the *impeller* (a centrifugal pump), *the turbine wheel* (or driven wheel) and *the fixed guide wheel* (or reaction wheel).

The diesel engine drives the impeller and its power is passed on to the oil in the converter. The oil is impelled by the impeller blades on to the turbine wheel blades, causing the turbine wheel to rotate.

The turbine wheel is connected by a shaft to the locomotive wheels. When the turbine wheel rotates, the locomotive wheels also rotate. The oil is returned by the turbine wheel blades to the impeller, passing through the blades of the fixed guide wheel which adjust the angle of flow of oil to the impeller. The oil is pumped round the circuit again and again.

Diesel locomotives having hydraulic transmission are called diesel-hydraulic locomotives.

Fluid Couplings.

Sometimes torque converters are used in conjunction with *fluid couplings*. These are similar to torque converters, but do not have a fixed guide wheel.

A fluid coupling is like a cushion of oil which smoothes the drive from the diesel engine and protects the engine from shocks transmitted back from the track by the locomotive driving wheels.

HYDRAULIC TRANSMISSION

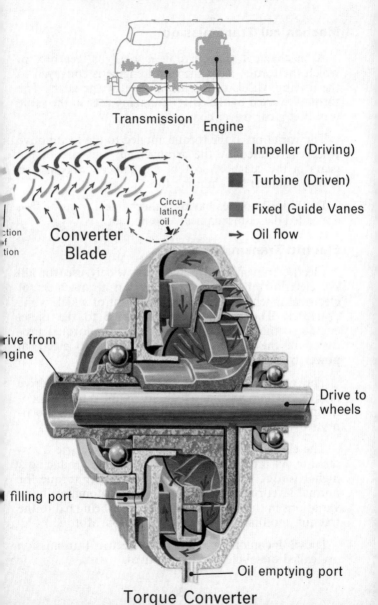

Transmission   Engine

Impeller (Driving)
Turbine (Driven)
Fixed Guide Vanes
→ Oil flow

Converter Blade

Circulating oil

Drive from engine

Drive to wheels

filling port

Oil emptying port

Torque Converter

Mechanical Transmission

A mechanical transmission is really a gearbox in which the torque from the diesel engine is conveyed to the driving wheels of the locomotive by the gears. The torque is varied by the driver changing gear in the same way that a car driver changes gear.

The variation in the torque applied to the locomotive wheels is limited by the arrangement and size of the gears in the gearbox, so that mechanical transmission is only suitable for shunting locomotives.

Diesel locomotives having a mechanical transmission are called diesel-mechanical locomotives.

Electric Transmission

Electric transmission is the most widely used of all. An electric transmission is simply an arrangement of electrical machines, the most important of which is the *generator*. The generator is connected to the diesel engine so that the mechanical power (or torque) produced in the diesel engine is converted to electrical power by the generator.

The electrical power is fed along cables to drive electric *traction motors*, which are coupled to the locomotive driving axles through gears to turn the locomotive wheels.

The electrical machines making up an electric transmission act rather like a torque converter, producing a higher torque for starting off, and a lower torque for normal level running. All this is done automatically by variations in the flow of electric current being fed to the traction motors. (See page 46 'Traction Motors'.)

Diesel locomotives having an electric transmission are called diesel-electric locomotives.

Mechanical Transmission

Electric Transmission

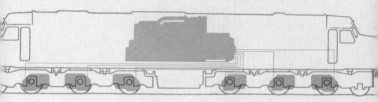

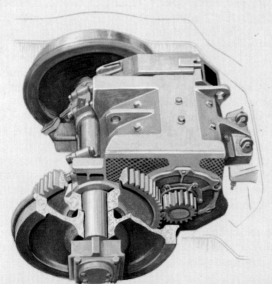

Traction Motor for electric transmission

How the Diesel Locomotive
makes use of Electricity

All diesel locomotives use electricity to perform various tasks. One of the most important of these is the operating of all the *auxiliary equipment*.

Two very important auxiliaries are the *compressor* (see page 38) and the *exhausters* (see page 38). Both of these are driven by electric motors, and are used to operate the brakes (see page 38). Also, electricity is used to provide lighting in the driver's cab and in the engine room. Sometimes electricity generated on the locomotive is used to light the carriages.

The *blowers*, which blow air into the traction motors to keep them cool, are also driven by electricity.

Each locomotive has a special generator, called the *auxiliary generator*, for producing electricity to operate all this auxiliary equipment. The auxiliary generator is driven by the diesel engine.

One of the most interesting ways in which electricity is used is in starting the diesel engine. All internal combustion engines, as in a car or a motor cycle, have to be started by an independent power supply before they can produce power of their own. With diesel electric locomotives having an electric transmission, the main generator which provides electrical power to drive the traction motor can be used as an electric motor to turn the diesel engine when starting it. The electric current required to do this is supplied by batteries which are kept in containers on each side of the locomotive.

The diesel engines in diesel mechanical and hydraulic locomotives are started by special motor/generators called 'dynostarters'.

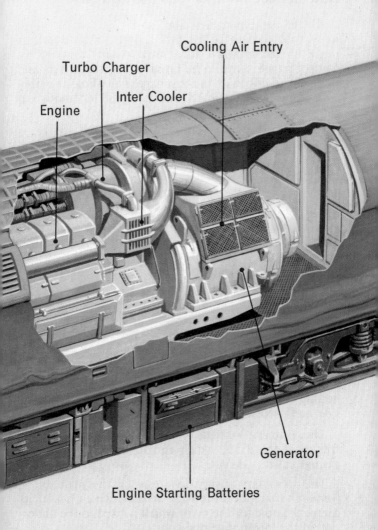

Cooling Air Entry

Turbo Charger

Inter Cooler

Engine

Generator

Engine Starting Batteries

How the Locomotive runs on the Track

All the equipment described so far, and many other items too, need to be assembled onto a framework to make up the complete locomotive. Cabs, with master control panels, have to be provided for the driver, and these are described on the next page. The whole assembly is then mounted on wheels to enable the locomotive to run on the track.

The wheels on main-line diesel locomotives are secured in *bogies*. Each locomotive has two bogies, one at each end, which are rather like carriages upon which the body of the locomotive is carried. Bogies can have two or three pairs of wheels, depending upon the size of the locomotive.

A locomotive needs bogies because it is so long that it would not go round the curves in the track if the wheels were fixed to the locomotive frame. A bogie carries equipment other than wheels; for example, the traction motors.

Not all the axles are driven by traction motors; some are 'idlers' which are there to help support the weight of the locomotive.

In each bogie there are a number of springs to smooth the ride of the locomotive and to stop it swaying too much at high speed. The springs of the bogie are usually arranged in two sets known as *primary suspension* and *secondary suspension*.

The primary suspension supports the main bogie frame on the axles, which run in bearings in special casings called *axleboxes*.

The secondary suspension rests on the main bogie frame and supports the *bogie bolster*, which has at its centre the hole for the pivot which is fixed to the underside of the locomotive body.

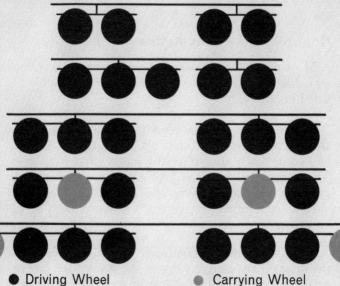

● Driving Wheel   ● Carrying Wheel

Wheel Arrangements

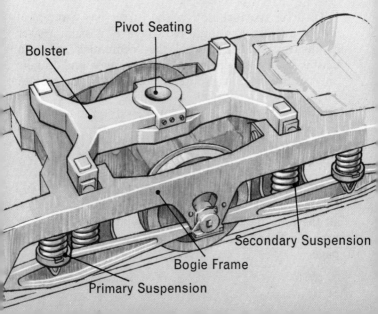

Pivot Seating

Bolster

Secondary Suspension

Bogie Frame

Primary Suspension

Controlling the Locomotive

Most diesel locomotives have a driver's cab at each end. Identical sets of controls and indicator lights are fitted in both cabs.

Everything in the cabs is compactly arranged so that the driver can work the controls, watch the track ahead *and* easily keep an eye on the gauges and indicators. The gauges tell him the locomotive speed, brake air pressure, vacuum reading and, in the case of diesel electric locomotives, the current being produced by the generator.

Indicator lights, coloured red, yellow and blue, show the driver if the engine stops, if the wheels are slipping or if a fault has developed in any part of the power equipment.

To drive the locomotive, the driver has a series of levers, handles and buttons. There is a main power handle to set and control the locomotive speed, a master handle which has forward, reverse and 'engine only' positions, and also handles to control the brakes. The diesel engine itself is stopped and started by pressing the 'engine off' or 'engine on' buttons.

There are a number of switches for various items of equipment.

There is a pedal which is part of the '*Driver's Safety Device*', which the driver keeps depressed with his foot all the time the locomotive is moving. This keeps the brakes off, and is explained in more detail on the next page.

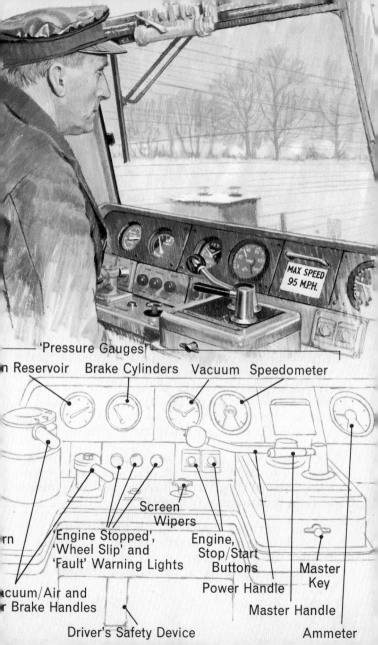

'Pressure Gauges'

Reservoir   Brake Cylinders   Vacuum   Speedometer

MAX SPEED
95 M.P.H.

Screen
Wipers

'Engine Stopped',
'Wheel Slip' and
'Fault' Warning Lights

Engine,
Stop/Start
Buttons

Master
Key

rn

cuum/Air and
r Brake Handles

Driver's Safety Device

Power Handle

Master Handle

Ammeter

How the Driver Brakes the Train

A train must have an efficient braking system, and two systems are generally used at the same time; compressed air-operated brakes for the locomotive and vacuum-operated brakes for the carriages or wagons.

The brakes on the locomotive and carriages or wagons are controlled by the driver from the locomotive cab.

The brakes are in the form of *shoes* which press against the rotating wheels and slow them by friction. A vacuum brake-pipe runs the length of the train, and the vacuum brakes fitted to the carriages and wagons are held in the 'off' position when a vacuum is created in the brake-pipe and in the *brake cylinders*, of which there is at least one on every vehicle. This is done by *exhausters* on the locomotive which draw air out of the brake-pipe and brake cylinders. To apply the brake, the driver admits air into the brake-pipe and brake cylinders by means of a brake valve. Inrushing air destroys the vacuum, and sets up a force in the brake cylinders powerful enough to operate the connecting levers and press the brake shoes against the wheels. This is a 'fail-safe' technique, since if the vacuum is destroyed for any reason—such as a broken brake-pipe or failure of a valve, air enters and applies the brake.

The pedal of a special safety device must be kept depressed by the driver's foot, otherwise a valve opens, letting in air. If the driver is ill and releases the pressure, the train is automatically braked.

The compressed air brakes on the locomotive are applied by air which is compressed in a *compressor* on the locomotive, and are operated by the same control valve that operates the vacuum brake on the rest of the train.

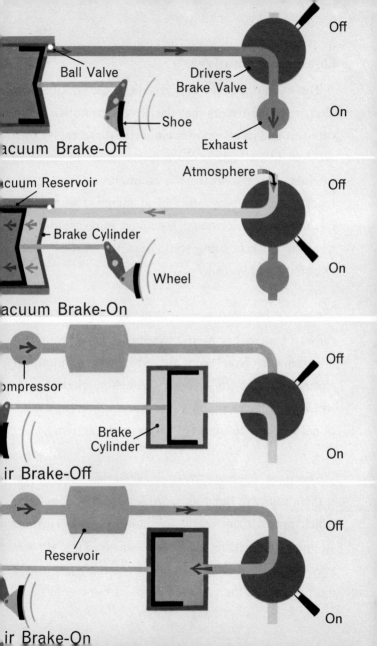

Ball Valve

Drivers Brake Valve

Off

On

Shoe

Exhaust

acuum Brake-Off

Atmosphere

Off

cuum Reservoir

Brake Cylinder

On

Wheel

acuum Brake-On

Off

ompressor

Brake Cylinder

On

ir Brake-Off

Off

Reservoir

On

ir Brake-On

Electric Locomotives

The main difference between diesel locomotives and electric locomotives is that the diesel locomotive has to carry around its own power plant (the diesel engine) *and* the fuel (diesel oil) to operate the plant in order to provide power to drive the locomotive. The electric locomotive is, on the other hand, supplied with power in the form of electricity, generated often many miles away in the generating stations of the normal public electricity grid system.

Electric locomotives can only be used where the railway system has been 'electrified'. This means that arrangements have been made to bring a supply of electricity to the track, either through an electric cable which runs high up above the track, or through additional rails which are used to conduct electricity.

The most important feature of electric locomotives is their ability to build up speed (or accelerate) quickly, which makes them useful for journeys which involve stopping and starting at a lot of stations. They are also very good for continuous high speed running on long journeys where there are few stops or none at all.

Power Supply

There are two types of electric current: alternating current (a.c.) in which the current flows first one way then the other in a forward and backward motion, and direct current (d.c.) which flows the same way all the time. The two types cannot be mixed. Power to operate the electric railways comes from the national grid system. The tall pylons you often see with their cables stretching across the country are part of this system, carrying high voltage alternating current.

Sub-stations are built at intervals along the railway track and these have *transformers* in which the high-voltage current from the grid is stepped down to about twenty-five thousand volts before being fed to the live rail or overhead wires from which the locomotive draws its power. This voltage is still too high for the traction motors, so it is stepped down again to about one thousand five hundred volts by another transformer in the locomotive. It can also be converted from a.c. to d.c. by a *rectifier*.

Pylon   Feeder Station   Cabin

1B36

Control Handle   Pantograph

Traction Motor   Rectifier   Control Equipment   Transformer

Power Protection and Collection

The electrical wiring of your home is protected by fuses which 'blow' if a fault develops and a piece of equipment becomes overloaded. Similarly, protection is needed in an electrified railway system where faults can occur for various reasons. It is also necessary for the effects of a fault to be confined to the shortest possible length of line, so that miles of track are not put out of action all at once. To provide this protection, cabins containing automatic switchgear are spaced along the track between the sub-stations. In this way a four or five mile section of line can be isolated.

Where the power supply is carried by a live steel rail supported on insulators running along the side of the track, iron shoes fitted to the locomotive slide along the rail, collect the electric current and pass it through cables to the traction motors.

Latest electrification systems, however, use overhead power supply wires. In this method, current is collected by a *pick-up* supported on a framework which keeps the pick-up in contact with the wire. The framework—known as a *pantograph*—automatically adjusts its running height to the varying height of the wire.

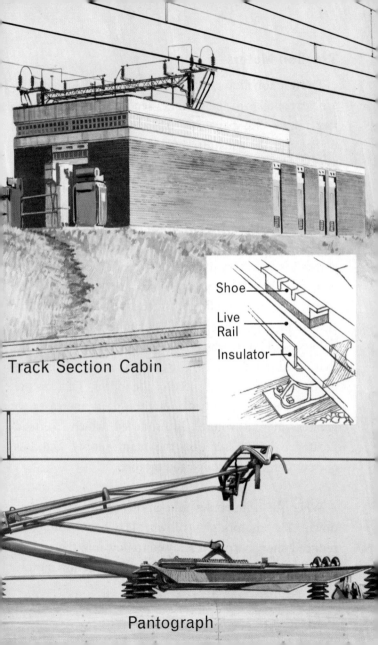

Track Section Cabin

Shoe
Live Rail
Insulator

Pantograph

Traction Motors

The traction motors which drive an electric locomotive are very similar to the motors used in the diesel-electric locomotive (see page 30). They are mounted in the bogies and the usual arrangement is that each driving axle has its own motor.

The driving power, or *tractive effort*, of a traction motor depends on, and is in proportion to, the current flowing through it. Great effort, and therefore high current, is necessary to start a train off from the station (see page 26, 'The mystery of Torque'). As it gathers speed, less tractive effort is needed. A feature of the electric motor is that while it is running it produces a voltage of its own which tries to push back the voltage that is being fed into it. The internal voltage is in proportion to the running speed of the motor. Thus, as the train speed increases, the motor speed increases, a greater internal voltage is produced which exerts a greater back pressure on the main supply and less current can flow through the motor.

When the train comes to a gradient it begins to slow down. The motors slow down. The back voltage is reduced, more current is allowed to flow into the motors and the tractive effort is increased. The traction motors therefore act as torque convertors.

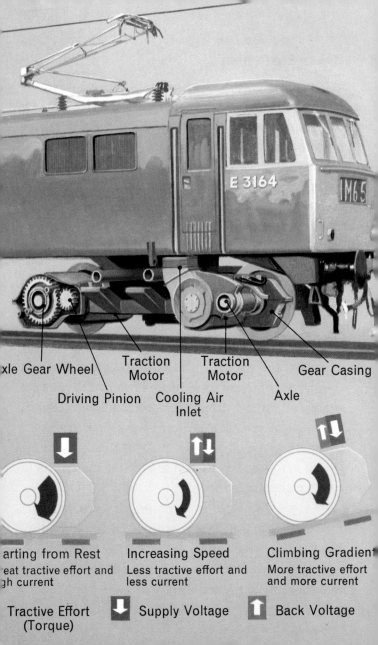

xle Gear Wheel   Traction Motor   Traction Motor   Gear Casing

Driving Pinion   Cooling Air Inlet   Axle

arting from Rest
eat tractive effort and
gh current

Increasing Speed
Less tractive effort and
less current

Climbing Gradien
More tractive effort
and more current

Tractive Effort (Torque)   Supply Voltage   Back Voltage

Power Equipment

We now know that electric locomotives are driven by means of traction motors which receive their electricity supply from an outside source through a live rail or overhead wire. This is only part of the story. Electric locomotives have a driving cab at each end, and the space between contains certain items of equipment essential to the functioning of the locomotive.

There is an electric motor-driven compressor to provide compressed air for the locomotive air brakes, the train vacuum brakes and some of the driving control gear. Electric fans are needed to blow cooling air through the hard-working traction motors. Transformers become hot with continually taking high-voltage electricity and stepping it down to pressures that will suit the traction motors: a pump is needed to circulate cooling oil around them. There are rectifiers to convert a.c. to d.c. A generator is required to charge the batteries and provide current for train lighting. A heating system must also be included to keep the train warm in cold weather.

All this equipment has to be carried on the locomotive. It will vary in detail design on different locomotives, but it is necessary in some form for the efficient operation of a modern electric train.

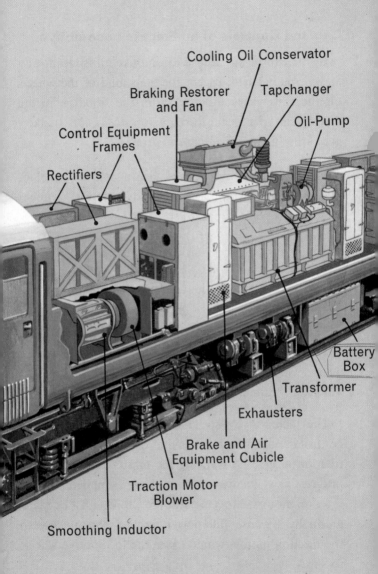

Cooling Oil Conservator

Braking Restorer and Fan

Tapchanger

Oil-Pump

Control Equipment Frames

Rectifiers

Battery Box

Transformer

Exhausters

Brake and Air Equipment Cubicle

Traction Motor Blower

Smoothing Inductor

B.R. Class A.L.6. Locomotive

Cab and Controls of an Electric Locomotive

In the cab of an electric locomotive all is clean, tidy and virtually silent, except for the sound of the wheels on the rails—very different from the situation in the driving cab of a steam locomotive with its coal bunker, perspiring fireman and general grime.

Electric locomotive drivers face a control panel of dials with plain and coloured sectors, gauges, switches and easily-operated controls.

There is an excellent view of the line ahead through wide cab windows fitted with windscreen wipers. As the driver sits controlling his train, he can tell from the instruments that every system of the locomotive is working satisfactorily. All the time the train is in motion, his foot is on the pedal of the driver's safety device which, as in the diesel locomotive, controls the 'fail-safe' braking mechanism.

The locomotive's speed is regulated by the master control handle, which varies the voltage being fed to the traction motors. Advancing the master control handle progressively increases the voltage supplied to the traction motors. Movement of the handle must be made gradually because full power applied too quickly to the traction motors would cause the locomotive wheels to slip.

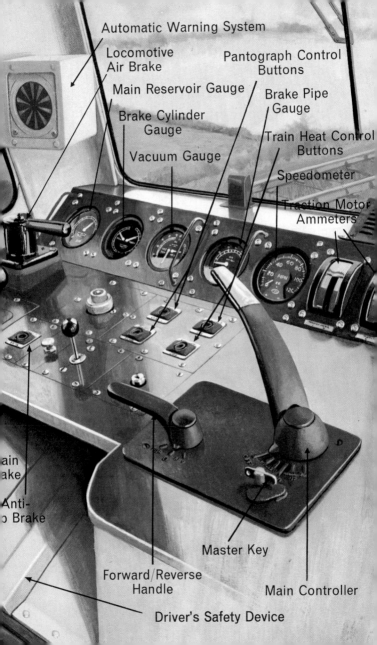

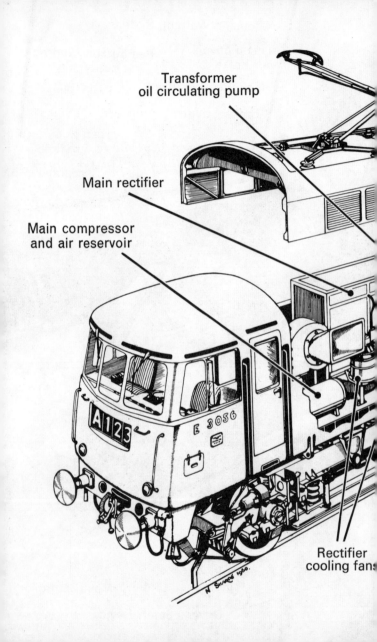

Transformer
oil circulating pump

Main rectifier

Main compressor
and air reservoir

A123

E 3056

Rectifier
cooling fans